TRICK OR TREAT!

a **MR. MEN™ LITTLE MISS™** book

originated by Roger Hargreaves

D0040414

Written and illustrated by Adam Hargreaves

Grosset & Dunlap

Mr. Happy decided to have a Halloween party!

A trick or treat party!

He spent an entire day decorating his house.

He hung bats and spiders and cobwebs from the ceiling.

There was even a witch in the fireplace.

Mr. Tickle helped out by carving as many pumpkins as he could find.

By the time the guests started to arrive, the lawn was filled with glowing jack-o'-lanterns.

Little Miss Magic was the first to arrive.

She dressed up as a witch and flew in on a broomstick.

Mr. Happy dressed up as a vampire to greet his friends.

Mr. Bump looked like he was wearing a mummy costume, but he'd actually just had a lot more bumps than usual that day.

When Little Miss Scary arrived, she immediately started playing tricks.

She scared the smile off Mr. Happy.

She scared the hat off Mr. Brave.

She even scared the bows off Little Miss Giggles.

Meanwhile, when Mr. Greedy arrived,
he immediately looked for treats.

There was a whole table full of them!

There was green-jelly slime, strawberry-jam
blood sandwiches, marshmallow ghosts, and
gingerbread skulls.

And everyone was excited to play party games!

Like bobbing for apples.

Mr. Noisy won easily.

He does have a very big mouth.

Mr. Clumsy did not easily win pin the tail on the witch's cat.

"Be careful, Mr. Clumsy!"

Just then, Mr. Happy noticed a guest he had forgotten to greet.

"You have a **vonderful** costume," he said in his best Dracula voice. "Now, who could it be?"

Everyone was very curious to figure out who the ghost was. They waited, ready to listen closely, but the ghost said nothing.

"Go on," Mr. Happy said to the ghost. "I give up, who are you?"

Wordlessly, the ghost rose up into the air. Little Miss Giggles giggled nervously.

"Oh my," she squeaked. "It's a real ghost!"

"Don't be silly," snorted Mr. Uppity. "There's no such thing."

The ghost did not like the sound of that. It laughed an eerie, hollow laugh and rattled its chains.

"Don't worry," said Mr. Tickle. "I bet it's Little Miss Scary playing a trick. I know just how to sort this out."

He reached out his extraordinarily long arms, but his fingers passed right through the ghost!

Everyone looked scared.

But not as scared as when they saw the ghost walk through the wall!

There was just the sheet left!

There was no one there.

Mr. Brave screamed a high-pitched scream that wasn't so brave.

Just when they thought Mr. Happy's house was haunted, Mr. Impossible appeared out of nowhere. "Boo!" he said, smiling.

"My goodness," laughed Mr. Happy. "That was quite the Halloween trick. You really had us scared!"

"I wasn't scared," said Little Miss Tiny as she crawled out from under the table.

Mr. Happy smiled at his friends. "I think we've had enough tricks for the night, now let's get to the treats!"

A monstrous roar came from the snack table.

"If Mr. Greedy left us any . . . Happy Halloween!"